A New Blanket for Josh

written by Phyllis Martin

illustrated by Gwen Connelly

Library of Congress Catalog Card Number 87-91995
Copyright ©1988, Phyllis Martin
Published by The STANDARD PUBLISHING Company, Cincinnati, Ohio
Division of STANDEX INTERNATIONAL Corporation. Printed in U.S.A.

"Mother, I'm home," Josh said, running up the walk. "And guess what? I can write my name. See." Josh waved some papers in the air.

"But, Josh, you already knew how to write your name."

"No, Mother, I knew how to *print* my name, now I can do both. *Write* and *print.*"

"Good for you, Son. Good for you. Now take your papers to your room. Inky's in there, asleep on your new blanket."

"A new blanket! Oh, Mother, I don't want a new blanket! I want Banklet, my old one," cried Josh.

"Calm down, Josh. It's just a lovely new blanket. It's really nice, and you like nice things, don't you?"

"Yes, I *like* nice things, but I *love* Banklet. Banklet's not a thing."

"Josh, dear, please say blanket and not Banklet."

"But Banklet's not a regular blanket. Banklet's special," Josh said, beginning to cry. Then his mother put her arms around him and hugged him close. She told Josh not to cry.

"I'm not crying. My eyes are just full of water. And some of it is spilling out."

"Never mind, Josh. Blanket—I mean Banklet—is so worn and really much too small for your new bed."

"But, Mother, you can't just throw Banklet away. Banklet's got feelings."

"Feelings? Blankets don't feel, Josh. How could Banklet have feelings?"

"Cause I gave him mine," said Josh.

"Oh, Josh," Mother said. "Listen for a minute. You know we love you, don't you?" Josh lifted his chin to keep more water from spilling out of his eyes.

"Yes," Josh whispered.

"And you know that we already had a little girl when you were born. But you were so special, we loved you right away. We didn't take our love from your sister Kelly and give it to you. We had more than enough for both of you. There's more love in this world than people ever use, Josh."

"And you can learn to love two blankets, just like we love two children. Don't you already love more than two people? You must, because you mention so many people in your prayers."

Josh nodded his head.

Mother went on, "I wasn't trying to get rid of Banklet, Josh. I just knew a bigger blanket was needed to cover a bigger boy—you."

"And you know what? I put some of my love feelings into your new blanket. I said to myself as I chose it, 'When I put this blanket over Josh tonight, I'll really be covering him with love.'"

"But, Mother, what did you do with Banklet? Where did you put him? Not outside! It's cold there."

"Now, Josh, calm down and listen to me. I didn't throw Banklet away. I put Banklet in the pretty see-through wrapper that came with your new blanket. If you go and look, you will see Banklet in that wrapper on the top shelf of your closet. And, Josh, if you truly care for Banklet, you won't use him every night. He's wearing out. See how frayed and small he's become? If you use him every night, there won't be anything left after a while. Why not save Banklet for special times such as Christmas and your birthday? That way, you'll have him for a long, long time."

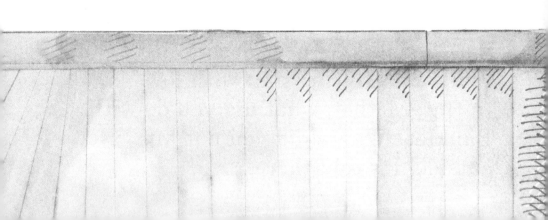

Josh didn't say anything. He just turned and headed for his room.

"And, Josh," Mother called after him, "look at Inky on your bed. See how he feels about your new blanket. Doesn't he look snug on it? And listen to that purr of his. It means he likes your new blanket, and he's happy to share it with you."

When Josh went to bed that night, he started to ask his mother to make it a special occasion so he could sleep with Banklet. Then PLOP! Inky landed on his bed and curled up into a soft, furry ball right on top of the new blanket!

Oh well, thought Josh, a big boy needs a big blanket.

He looked at his mother and said, "Guess I'll choose the new blanket tonight. It has feelings too. Your love feelings."

"Yes, it does," Mother agreed with a smile. "But now, Josh, let me hear your new prayer about love."

Josh began to pray,

"The Bible in one word is LOVE.
Lord, help us learn love's way.
Let it light up all our nights
And brighten every day. Amen."

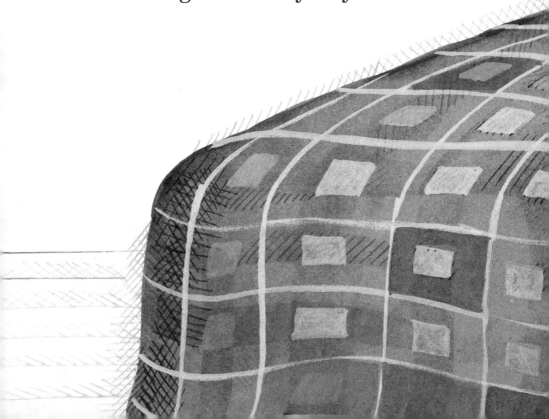

As Mother tiptoed away, she whispered, "Josh, if you have any trouble getting used to your new blanket, tell God about it. He's always awake and ready to listen."